Violet
the Painting
Fairy

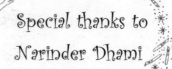

Special thanks to
Narinder Dhami

ORCHARD BOOKS
338 Euston Road, London NW1 3BH
Orchard Books Australia
Level 17/207 Kent Street, Sydney, NSW 2000
A Paperback Original

First published in 2014 by Orchard Books

HiT entertainment

A CIP catalogue record for this book is available
from the British Library.

ISBN 978 1 40833 149 1

1 3 5 7 9 10 8 6 4 2

Printed in Great Britain

The paper and board used in this paperback are natural recyclable
products made from wood grown in sustainable forests. The
manufacturing processes conform to the environmental regulations
of the country of origin.

Orchard Books is a division of Hachette Children's Books,
an Hachette UK company

www.hachette.co.uk

Violet
the Painting
Fairy

by Daisy Meadows

ORCHARD

www.rainbowmagic.co.uk

The Fairyland Palace

Bridge

Sara Sketchley's house

Rainspell

Island

Maze

Park

Carys's Jewellery Shop

Beach and Promenade

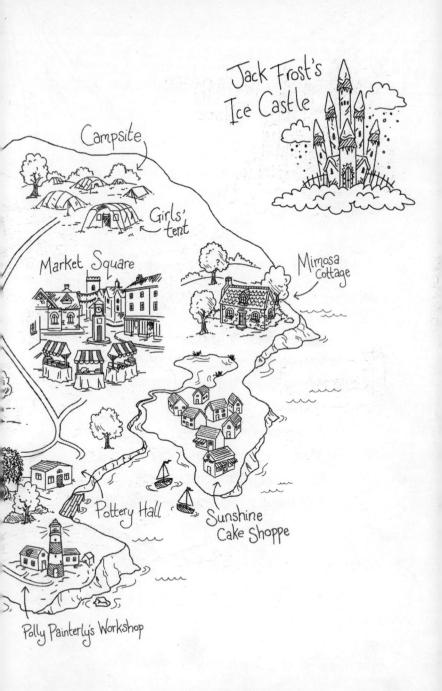

Jack Frost's
Ice Castle

Campsite

Girls'
tent

Mimosa
Cottage

Market Square

Pottery Hall

Sunshine
Cake Shoppe

Polly Painterly's Workshop

Jack Frost's Spell

I'm a wonderful painter, you must have heard of me,
Marvel at my amazing artistic ability!
With palette, brush and paints in hand,
I'll be the most famous artist in the land!

The Magical Crafts Fairies can't stop me,
I'll steal their magic and then you'll see
That everyone, whatever the cost,
Will want a painting by Jack Frost!

Contents

Paint Mix-up!

"We're not far from the lighthouse now, Kirsty," said Rachel. The two girls were walking along the cliff path towards the headland where the Rainspell Island lighthouse stood. "Dad said we can't miss it! I wonder what he meant?"

"We'll soon find out!" Kirsty replied.

"I'm so glad we came
to Rainspell for
another holiday,
Rachel. There
isn't anywhere
else like it in the
whole world!"

The girls were
spending the spring
holiday on Rainspell Island, and they
were taking it in turns to stay with
Kirsty's mum and dad at their bed and
breakfast one night, and then at the
campsite with Rachel's parents the next.

"It's an extra-special holiday
because it's Rainspell Crafts Week,"
Rachel pointed out. "*And* because
of our adventures with the Magical
Crafts Fairies!"

When the girls arrived on Rainspell,
Kayla the Pottery Fairy, one of the
Magical Crafts Fairies, had invited them
to Fairyland where a Crafts Week was
also taking place. The Magical Crafts
Fairies were organising the event, and
Kayla told the girls that King Oberon
and Queen Titania would be choosing
the most beautiful crafts to decorate their
royal palace.

But as the queen welcomed everyone
to the start of Crafts Week, Jack Frost
and his naughty goblins had hurled
paint-filled balloons into the crowd. The
Magical Crafts Fairies and even Queen
Titania herself had been splattered with
bright green paint. In the chaos that
followed, Rachel and Kirsty had been
dismayed to discover that Jack Frost and

his goblins had stolen the Magical Crafts Fairies' special objects, the source of their powerful magic.

Jack Frost had declared that *he* was the best artist ever, and he'd taken the magical objects to make sure that no one else could ever be better than him. Then, as everyone watched helplessly, Jack Frost had whisked himself and his goblins magically away from Fairyland to hide themselves and the magical objects in the human world. The fairies had been very distressed, but Rachel and Kirsty had stepped forward instantly to offer their help. The girls were determined to prevent Crafts Weeks everywhere, in both the human and the fairy worlds, from turning into complete disasters.

"Thank goodness we've already

found Kayla's vase, Annabelle's pencil sharpener, Zadie's thimble and Josie's beads," Kirsty said. "I really enjoyed our pottery, drawing, sewing and jewellery-making workshops."

"Me too," Rachel agreed. "But they would have been ruined if the fairies hadn't got their magical objects back just in time!"

Kirsty nodded. "I can't wait to try Polly Painterly's class at the lighthouse today," she said eagerly. "Painting is one of my *very* favourite things."

"But what will the class be like, now that Violet the Painting Fairy doesn't have her magical paintbrush?" Rachel asked anxiously.

"Well, as Queen Titania always says, we just have to wait for the magic to come to us!" Kirsty reminded her.

Suddenly Rachel spotted the lighthouse ahead of them.

"*Now* I see what Dad meant when he said we couldn't miss it!" she laughed. The lighthouse was painted in bold blue and white stripes and the top, which housed the lamp, was a bright crimson.

"I read in the Crafts Week brochure that Polly Painterly is the lighthouse keeper, as well as a famous local artist," Kirsty said as they approached the colourful building.

"She must be pretty busy, then!"
Rachel remarked. There was a sign
pinned to the door – *Painting Class in
the Lantern Room today*. The girls went
inside and began climbing the spiral
staircase. The walls were lined with
watercolour paintings of Rainspell, all
signed *Polly Painterly*.

"These are lovely," Kirsty said. "Look, Rachel, this is the wood where we met Ruby the Red Fairy."

"Our very first fairy adventure!" Rachel said with a smile.

The first thing Rachel and Kirsty noticed when they entered the lantern room was the stunning view. Through the enormous window that ran all the way around the circular room, they could see sailing boats bobbing on the sea, golden beaches backed by white cliffs, the village with its picturesque little cottages and the rolling, green countryside.

A group of children wearing painting smocks were standing behind easels, waiting for the class to start. Meanwhile, a young woman with streaks of vivid pink in her blonde hair was giving out palettes, brushes and tubes of paint.

"Hi, girls," the young woman called, "I'm Polly Painterly. Come and join us!"

"I'm Kirsty and this is Rachel," Kirsty explained, noticing that there were lots more paintings propped against the walls of the lantern room. "We were just admiring the view!"

"Wonderful, isn't it?" Polly sighed happily. "It inspires all my work." She gave the girls painting materials and smocks to protect their clothes, then clapped her hands for silence.

"Welcome to Rainspell Lighthouse," Polly said. "I can't wait to show you how much fun painting can be!

First we're going to mix some colours. Let's start with yellow and blue, then we'll try yellow and red. Can anyone guess what colours those will make?"

"Yellow and blue make green," Kirsty said, remembering something she'd learned at school.

"And yellow and red make orange," a boy next to Rachel added.

Polly showed everyone how to squeeze the paints onto their palettes and mix them with their brushes. But Kirsty was dismayed that her yellow and blue mixture ended up a sludgy grey colour, not green.

19

Then she tried swirling the yellow and red paint together, but that instantly turned grey, too.

"This is dreadful!" Rachel groaned, pulling a face. "All I get is grey!"

The other children were having the same problem, and Polly looked very bewildered. "Try mixing red and white," she suggested. "You should get pink."

Everyone did so, but once again all the mixtures turned a dull grey. The paint was also very thin, and it began to dribble off the palettes onto the floor, making a real mess.

"Why is *everything* going wrong?"
Polly wondered, frowning. The girls
glanced knowingly at each other. This
was all because of Jack Frost!

"It must be a bad batch of paint,"
Polly decided. "I'll fetch some more and
clean all the brushes, too. While I'm
gone, have a look at my paintings to
get some ideas for your own pictures."
And, clutching the dirty brushes, she
disappeared down the spiral staircase.

"What a disaster, Kirsty," Rachel whispered as they studied a painting of a sailing boat. "With Violet's magical paintbrush missing, our pictures will be terrible!"

Kirsty peered closely at Polly's painting. "Rachel," she whispered, her voice full of suppressed excitement, "see that strange, glowing light on the tip of the sail in the picture?"

"What is it?" Rachel breathed, eyes wide.

As the girls watched, the light

headed directly towards them, and then it became a little fairy who fluttered right out of the painting.

"It's Violet!" Kirsty whispered. "Violet the Painting Fairy!"

Amazing
Artist

Rachel and Kirsty moved closer together
to hide Violet from the others as she flew
towards them. The little fairy winked
cheekily at them. She was dressed in
denim dungarees with the legs rolled up,
a colourful stripy top and purple boots.
Her dark ponytail was fixed in place
with a tiny paintbrush.

"Hello, girls," Violet whispered. "As you already know, yellow and blue should *not* make dirty grey! All my beautiful paint colours are spoilt now that Jack Frost has my magic paintbrush. Will you help me get it back?"

"Of course we will!" Rachel agreed instantly. Violet beamed at the girls but then a look of alarm crossed her face. The other children were making their way towards the sailing-boat picture. Without another word, Violet dived headfirst into the pocket of Kirsty's smock and disappeared from view.

26

"I really like this picture," said one of the boys. "The sea looks so real."

"Yes, it's almost as if you can dive right into the waves," Kirsty agreed.

"Polly's paintings are brilliant," another girl remarked. "I love this one of the beach in winter."

"Me too," said Rachel.

"Rubbish!" a scornful voice piped up behind them. "Polly's paintings aren't so great. I can paint a million times better than that!"

Everyone spun around in surprise.

27

Kirsty and Rachel saw a boy wearing a long painting smock and a baseball cap standing at an easel on the other side of the room. He twirled his paintbrush expertly in one hand while glaring at Kirsty, Rachel and the others.

"Really?" Rachel asked. "Prove it, then! Can we see your picture?"

The boy shrugged. "I've only just started," he replied. "But yes, come and watch a painting genius at work!"

Rachel and Kirsty went over to his easel, followed by the other children. The boy's canvas was almost blank, except for a blue wash at the top. But as everyone watched his confident brushstrokes, the painting began to take shape. Rachel quickly realised that the boy was doing a self-portrait of himself, with the seaside in the background.

"This painting is brilliant!" Rachel murmured to Kirsty as the boy added some seagulls flying through the clouds. "You can almost see each grain of golden sand."

"And the waves look like they're rolling right off the picture," Kirsty added. The only odd thing was that the boy had painted himself with *very* large feet. Kirsty glanced down and gasped when she saw the big feet tucked under the easel.

"You must be gasping with amazement at my wonderful painting!" the boy said smugly.

"Er—yes!" Kirsty agreed. She nudged Rachel. "Look at his feet," Kirsty whispered to her friend. "I think he might be a goblin!"

Then Rachel noticed something, too – a few long strands of long icy hair poking out of the top of the painting smock.

"It's not a goblin, Kirsty," Rachel whispered back. "It's Jack Frost himself!"

Then Kirsty felt a tiny hand tugging at her sleeve.

"Jack Frost is using my magical paintbrush to paint his picture!" Violet murmured indignantly. Kirsty peered a little closer and saw a very fine, faint haze of shimmering magic around the brush.

At that moment Polly Painterly hurried back into the lantern room. "I have new paint and clean brushes for everyone," she announced.

The other children rushed over to collect their new materials. Meanwhile, Kirsty and Rachel confronted Jack Frost.

"We know you have Violet the Painting Fairy's magical brush!" Kirsty said, staring sternly at him. "She'd like it back, please."

"No way!" Jack Frost declared with an icy sneer. "I love painting pictures, especially of myself, and I have a wonderful gallery of self-portraits back at my Ice Castle. I intend to paint many, many more, and no pesky fairies or silly human girls are going to stop me!"

Then, clutching the paintbrush, he dodged around the girls and ran off down the spiral staircase.

"Quick, Kirsty!" Rachel said urgently. "He mustn't get away!"

A Rogues' Gallery

Quickly the girls slipped out of the lantern room. No one noticed because Polly was still giving out fresh supplies to the other children.

"It might be quicker if Violet turns us into fairies," Kirsty panted as they hurried down the stairs.

"Great idea," Violet agreed, but suddenly they heard a familiar voice below them call "Hello, girls!" Rachel and Kirsty glanced down and saw Artie Johnson, the Crafts Week organiser, coming up the winding stairs. With a squeak of alarm, Violet ducked down again into Kirsty's pocket.

"Hello, Artie," said Rachel as both girls stopped to let her pass. Jack Frost

was getting away, Rachel realised, but that couldn't be helped.

"We're really enjoying Crafts Week," Kirsty added.

Artie beamed at them. "I'm glad to hear it," she replied, "And I'm also glad to see that *some* children, like you, have delightful manners, unlike that extremely rude boy who just pushed past me!"

Kirsty and Rachel glanced at each other. *Jack Frost!*

"I'm here to check on the painting class," Artie went on. "You're not leaving already, are you?"

Rachel thought fast. "We'll be back in a little while," she replied. "We've remembered that we – er – have something important to do first."

"See you later," Artie said, and headed

to the lantern room. The girls could see the whole of the spiral staircase below them, but Jack Frost had vanished.

"What now?" Kirsty asked, dismayed, as Violet popped out of her pocket.

"Remember what Jack Frost said about the art gallery at his Ice Castle?" Rachel recalled. "Maybe he's gone there."

"It's worth a try!" Violet agreed hopefully. With one twirl of her wand, she transformed the girls into tiny winged fairies. Then Violet waved her wand once more, and a cloud of dazzling, magical sparkles whirled them all away to Jack Frost's Ice Castle.

Just a few seconds later, Violet, Rachel and Kirsty found themselves in Jack Frost's art gallery.

It was an enormous room, and the frozen walls were crammed with paintings displayed in frames of carved ice. All the pictures were of Jack Frost in  various poses with different props. There were palettes, blank canvases and tubes of paint lying everywhere.

"Look, there he is!" Kirsty whispered as the three friends flew to land on top of one of the picture frames.

Jack Frost was perched on a stool at an easel in the middle of the room. He had Violet's magical paintbrush in his hand and he was painting yet another picture of himself, this time sitting in state on his ice throne. The goblins, wearing green smocks and berets, were being kept busy framing and hanging the pictures.

Rachel looked down and noticed that
there was a big pile of paintings still
waiting to be framed. A group of goblins
were carving the frames as fast as they
could, chipping away at blocks of ice.

"These pictures are boring!" one of
the goblins complained to the others.
"They're all of Jack Frost! Why won't he
paint any pictures of *us*?"

"He says we're not handsome enough!"
another goblin grumbled.

"Jack Frost won't let us have a go with the magical paintbrush either," said the goblin next to him. "He's really mean!"

The goblins' conversation sparked off an idea in Kirsty's head. She whispered to Rachel and Violet, and the three of them flew out of the gallery into the empty corridor outside.

"The goblins have a lot of work to do," Kirsty pointed out, her eyes twinkling. "I think they need some help! Violet, could you disguise me and Rachel as goblins?"

Violet frowned. "Yes, but you know I don't have *all* my magical powers without my paintbrush," she replied. "And goblin disguises use a whole lot of magic!"

"We'll be quick," Kirsty promised.

"I think I know how we can get the paintbrush back!"

Violet nodded. She waved her wand, surrounding the girls with a magical ring of fairy sparkles.

The girls had been disguised as goblins before, but Kirsty still got a shock when she looked down at her hands and saw them turning bright green! Rachel was turning the same shade of green, and her nose, ears and feet were growing bigger. Kirsty felt her own nose and ears – they were *enormous*.

43

"You both look very goblin-like!"
Violet giggled as the girls hurried back
into the gallery. "Good luck!"

"I keep tripping over my massive feet!"
Rachel murmured as she and Kirsty went
over to Jack Frost. He was just about to
begin a new painting.

"Shall I clean your brush before you
start?" Kirsty offered hopefully. But Jack
Frost didn't even look at her.

"Get me a fresh jar of water," he
ordered. Rachel dashed off to fetch it.

"What about your brush?" asked
Kirsty. "It looks very dirty."

"I'm out of blue paint," Jack Frost
snapped, throwing the empty tube on the
floor. "Bring me some immediately!"

Kirsty rummaged through the nearest
heap of paints and found a tube of blue.

Jack Frost snatched it from her, then grabbed the water from Rachel.

"I could clean your brush quickly while you decide what to paint," said Rachel innocently.

Jack Frost ignored her. He dunked the magical paintbrush in the water, squeezed the blue paint onto the palette and began painting again with swift, sure strokes. The girls exchanged a look of frustration.

"You know, your brush really *does* need cleaning –" Kirsty began.

"Fetch me some white paint!" Jack Frost shouted, still clutching the paintbrush tightly. "I *must* finish this painting!"

For the next ten minutes Jack Frost sent the girls on a variety of errands while he painted a picture of himself in the Ice Castle gardens. But, to their dismay, he ignored all their requests to clean his paintbrush.

46

At last Jack Frost gave a sigh of relief. "Finished!" he announced. For the first time he glanced at Kirsty and Rachel, and his icy brows drew together in a thunderous scowl.

"And *who* are *you*?" said Jack Frost suspiciously.

With a feeling of dread, Kirsty glanced down at her hands. The bright green colour was fading. Violet's magic was wearing off!

"Goblins!" Jack Frost shrieked furiously. "Lock these pesky fairies up in the dungeons *immediately*!"

Rainbow Fairies

As the goblins charged towards them, Rachel grabbed a big armful of tubes of paint.

"Help me, Kirsty!" she shouted.

"You don't have time to paint a picture!" Jack Frost sneered. "You're under arrest!" But realising what Rachel was planning, Kirsty scooped up a pile

of paints herself. Then the girls whipped
the tops off the tubes and began squirting
paint at the advancing goblins. Blobs of
yellow, blue and red paint flew through
the air, splattering the goblins all over.
The goblins stopped in their tracks. Then
they burst out laughing.

"Paint fight! Paint fight!" they chorused
gleefully. Grabbing handfuls of the tubes,
they began squirting paint at each other

and whooping with delight.

"I order you to capture these silly fairies!" Jack Frost yelled as the girls flew towards the door, but the goblins were having far too much fun to listen to him. Paint was flying in all directions.

Rachel could see that the gallery floor was already covered in streaks of different colours – red, orange, yellow, green, blue, indigo and violet.

"The floor looks like a rainbow," Rachel remarked to Kirsty as they hurried out into the corridor where

51

Violet was waiting.

"Yes, it's the same colours as the Rainbow Fairies," Kirsty agreed. Then she clapped a hand to her mouth in excitement. "Rachel, that's *exactly* who we need to help us get the magical paintbrush back!"

"I'm thinking the same thing!" Rachel said as Violet flew to join them. Quickly the girls explained their idea, and a happy smile lit up Violet's face.

"Fairyland, here we come!" she declared.
As they flew towards the corridor
window Kirsty and Rachel heard Jack
Frost screech at the goblins, "Stop this
nonsense RIGHT NOW!"

The girls grinned and followed Violet
out of the Ice Castle into the dark, frozen
countryside that surrounded it.

A short while later, the three friends
reached the blue skies and warm
sunshine of Fairyland. Below them Kirsty
and Rachel could see the pink towers
of the royal palace, the toadstool houses
and the winding river.

As they swooped lower, they saw
the Rainbow Fairies in one of the
wildflower meadows. Kirsty peered down
and realised the fairies were playing a
skipping game.

53

"Look at their colourful skipping rope!" Kirsty exclaimed. "It's like a rainbow when it swings around."

Fern the Green Fairy and Amber the Orange Fairy were holding the ends of the rope and turning it while the other five fairies skipped together, singing:

We're the Rainbow Fairies,
Colourful as can be,
Colours here, colours there,

Rainbow colours everywhere!

Suddenly Ruby the Red Fairy glanced up and spotted them.

"It's Violet, Rachel and Kirsty!" Ruby called. The other Rainbow Fairies looked up, too, and immediately got into a muddle with their skipping rope. Laughing, the fairies untangled themselves and rushed to greet Violet and the girls.

"Rainbow Fairies, we really need your help," Rachel said, and quickly she explained what had happened at Jack Frost's Ice Castle.

"Will you come?" Kirsty added.

"Try and stop us!" declared Izzy the Indigo Fairy with a grin.

Colour Confusion

Violet, Rachel and Kirsty led the way
back to the Ice Castle with the Rainbow
Fairies flying close behind them. They
all slipped through the corridor window,
then Rachel, Kirsty and Violet peeped
into the gallery.

"What a mess!" Rachel whispered.

The goblins were still running about squirting paint at each other. They were all covered in streaks of different colours from their heads to their enormous feet. The floor was now awash with puddles of paint, and some of the goblins were sliding around in it.

In the middle of the chaos, Jack Frost sat hunched over his easel. He was working on a new canvas, and Kirsty could see that this painting was bigger

than any of the others. She felt a little
sorry for Jack Frost who was trying to
ignore the goblins as he concentrated on
his picture.

"I told you lot before," Jack Frost
shouted furiously as a blob of green paint
 whizzed past his ear,
"you'd better not
spoil any of my
precious paintings,
or you'll be in big
trouble!"

Silently Violet
pointed at
Jack Frost's easel and beckoned to the
others. Rachel, Kirsty and the fairies flew
across the room, dodging the flying paint
and keeping out of sight. Then they all
hid behind the easel.

"I need that special shade of ice blue to paint my cape," Jack Frost muttered, beginning to rummage through the tubes of paint lying next to him.

Hearing this gave Rachel an idea. Swiftly she outlined her plan to the others, and the Rainbow Fairies nodded, holding their wands aloft.

"Get ready," Ruby the Red Fairy whispered. "One, two, THREE!"

On the count of three, all the Rainbow Fairies waved their wands and glittering clouds of rainbow-coloured

fairy dust billowed around the room.

"Look at the paintings, Kirsty!" Rachel said with a smile.

The pictures on the walls were changing colour before their very eyes. A painting of an orange sunset had now turned green and a painting of a deep blue sea had become bright red. In the paintings Jack Frost had been doing earlier, his ice throne was now purple, and his Ice Castle was a vivid pink.

But Kirsty and Rachel could see that the biggest change was in the portraits of Jack Frost himself.

"Hee hee hee!" one of the goblins chuckled, suddenly noticing the painting nearest him. "See how funny Jack Frost looks in this picture – he's got a green nose and orange hair! Ha ha ha!"

The other goblins stopped squirting paint and stared curiously at the paintings around them.

"His beard's indigo-coloured and his cape is bright red, not icy blue," another goblin chortled.

"And look at this painting of him with his wand!" a third goblin pointed out, "His magical ice bolts are primrose-yellow – ho ho ho!"

Jack Frost looked very upset. "Stop that!" he shrieked as the goblins rolled around on the floor, laughing

hysterically and getting covered in even more paint. "You'll pay for this, you giggling fools!"

At a sign from Violet, all the fairies whizzed out from behind the easel. Jack Frost was so shocked, he almost fell off his stool.

"The Rainbow Fairies will change the colours of the paintings back to how they should be," Rachel told him. "But *only* if you return the magical paintbrush to Violet right away!"

Picture Perfect

Jack Frost's face fell.

"I'm not giving up the magical paintbrush!" he snapped. But as the goblins continued to laugh themselves silly, wheezing and gasping for breath, Jack Frost frowned.

"Are you sure?" Violet asked him, her eyes twinkling.

Jack Frost groaned. "Here, take it!"

he mumbled, thrusting the paintbrush towards Violet. The instant Violet's fingers touched the handle of the brush, it shrank down to its tiny Fairyland size. The girls and the Rainbow Fairies applauded happily.

"At last!" Violet sighed with relief, waving the paintbrush in the air like a wand.

"Don't forget *your* side of the bargain!" Jack Frost reminded her crossly.

Rachel and Kirsty watched as the seven Rainbow Fairies conjured up their sparkling magic once again, and showers of rainbow fairy dust transformed the paintings back to their true colours. The goblins stopped laughing and picked themselves up off the floor.

"And this is for you," Violet told them. She pointed her wand at an empty space on the gallery wall and suddenly a new picture in an ice frame appeared. The girls grinned at each other when they saw it was a painting of three goblins. The goblins squealed with joy.

"What nonsense!" Jack Frost snorted, but Kirsty thought he

actually looked quite pleased.

"Girls, thank you once again," Violet said as the fairies left the gallery. "I really didn't believe we were *ever* going to get my paintbrush off Jack Frost!"

"We couldn't have done it without the Rainbow Fairies," Kirsty pointed out.

"We make a great team!" Sky the Blue Fairy laughed.

"It's time for us all to return to Fairyland," Violet went on, "and you

girls have a painting class to go to!" She raised her wand. "Goodbye, girls, and thank you for being such loyal friends."

"Goodbye," called the Rainbow Fairies as Kirsty and Rachel were swept away in a mist of fairy magic.

Seconds later the girls found themselves back in the Rainspell lighthouse, standing by the spiral staircase outside the lantern room. They hurried inside and found that the class was just about to start again.

"I'm really looking forward to seeing your pictures, everyone," Artie was saying to the others.

"Me too," agreed Polly Painterly. "Now, let's all try mixing those colours together again."

This time the painting class got off to a flying start as everyone, including the girls, mixed up beautiful shades of green, orange and pink. As they began painting, Polly and Artie moved around the easels,

giving everyone advice. Rachel chose
to paint a view of the beach, but Kirsty
wanted to do something different.

"Kirsty, that's a wonderful picture!"
Polly exclaimed a little later. Kirsty had
painted a portrait of Rachel with a
shimmering rainbow overhead.

"It's really good, Kirsty," Rachel said
admiringly, leaning
across from her
own easel
to take
a look.

"You
know, you
should
enter your
painting in the
competition on

the last day of Crafts Week," Artie told Kirsty. "That rainbow looks incredibly realistic – the colours simply glow!"

The girls glanced at each other.

"The rainbow reminds me of our fairy friends," Kirsty whispered as Artie moved away. "I'm just so glad we were able to help Violet today. And wasn't it great to meet the Rainbow Fairies again?"

Rachel nodded. "And I wonder which fairy will need our help tomorrow!" she said eagerly.

The End

**Now it's time for Kirsty and
Rachel to help...**

Libby the Story-Writing Fairy

Read on for a sneak peek...

"I wish I could paint like you, Kirsty!"
Rachel said, holding her friend's picture
up so she could admire it. The two girls
had attended a painting workshop at
Rainspell Lighthouse the day before.
"Mum, don't you think this painting is
really good?"

Mrs Walker was sitting in a deckchair
outside their tent, soaking up the
sunshine. She smiled and nodded.
"You're very talented, Kirsty," Mrs
Walker declared, taking the canvas to
have a closer look. "You've got Rachel's
hair and eye colour exactly right, and

that rainbow arching over her head looks beautiful."

"Thanks!" Kirsty laughed. "Artie Johnson, the Crafts Week organiser, told me I should enter it in the competition tomorrow."

Read **Libby the Story-Writing Fairy** to find out what adventures are in store for Kirsty and Rachel!

RAINBOW magic

Join in the magic online by signing up to the Rainbow Magic fan club!

Sign up today at:
www.rainbowmagicbooks.co.uk

Meet the
Magical Crafts Fairies

Kayla the Pottery Fairy

Annabelle the Drawing Fairy

Zadie the Sewing Fairy

Josie the Jewellery-Making Fairy

Violet the Painting Fairy

Libby the Story-Writing Fairy

Roxie the Baking Fairy

Jack Frost has stolen the Magical Crafts Fairies' special objects. Can Kirsty and Rachel help get them back before Rainspell Island's Crafts Week is ruined?

Competition!

The Magical Crafts Fairies have created a special
competition just for you!
In the back of each book in the Magical Crafts series there
will be a question for you to answer.
First you need to collect the answer from the back
of each book in the series.
Once you have all the answers, take the first letter from
each one and arrange them to spell a secret word!
When you have the answer, go online and enter!

What is the King of Fairyland called?

_ _ _ _ _ _

We will put all the correct entries into a draw and select
a winner to receive a special Rainbow Magic Goody Bag
featuring lots of treats for you and your fairy friends.
You'll also star in a new Rainbow Magic story!

Enter online now at www.rainbowmagicbooks.co.uk

Have you read them all?

The Rainbow Fairies
1. Ruby the Red Fairy ☐
2. Amber the Orange Fairy ☐
3. Saffron the Yellow Fairy ☐
4. Fern the Green Fairy ☐
5. Sky the Blue Fairy ☐
6. Izzy the Indigo Fairy ☐
7. Heather the Violet Fairy ☐

The Weather Fairies
8. Crystal the Snow Fairy ☐
9. Abigail the Breeze Fairy ☐
10. Pearl the Cloud Fairy ☐
11. Goldie the Sunshine Fairy ☐
12. Evie the Mist Fairy ☐
13. Storm the Lightning Fairy ☐
14. Hayley the Rain Fairy ☐

The Party Fairies
15. Cherry the Cake Fairy ☐
16. Melodie the Music Fairy ☐
17. Grace the Glitter Fairy ☐
18. Honey the Sweet Fairy ☐
19. Polly the Party Fun Fairy ☐
20. Phoebe the Fashion Fairy ☐
21. Jasmine the Present Fairy ☐

The Jewel Fairies
22. India the Moonstone Fairy ☐
23. Scarlett the Garnet Fairy ☐
24. Emily the Emerald Fairy ☐
25. Chloe the Topaz Fairy ☐
26. Amy the Amethyst Fairy ☐
27. Sophie the Sapphire Fairy ☐
28. Lucy the Diamond Fairy ☐

The Pet Keeper Fairies
29. Katie the Kitten Fairy ☐
30. Bella the Bunny Fairy ☐
31. Georgia the Guinea Pig Fairy ☐
32. Lauren the Puppy Fairy ☐
33. Harriet the Hamster Fairy ☐
34. Molly the Goldfish Fairy ☐
35. Penny the Pony Fairy ☐

The Fun Day Fairies
36. Megan the Monday Fairy
37. Tallulah the Tuesday Fairy
38. Willow the Wednesday Fairy
39. Thea the Thursday Fairy
40. Freya the Friday Fairy
41. Sienna the Saturday Fairy
42. Sarah the Sunday Fairy

The Petal Fairies
43. Tia the Tulip Fairy
44. Pippa the Poppy Fairy
45. Louise the Lily Fairy
46. Charlotte the Sunflower Fairy
47. Olivia the Orchid Fairy
48. Danielle the Daisy Fairy
49. Ella the Rose Fairy

The Dance Fairies
50. Bethany the Ballet Fairy
51. Jade the Disco Fairy
52. Rebecca the Rock'n'Roll Fairy
53. Tasha the Tap Dance Fairy
54. Jessica the Jazz Fairy
55. Saskia the Salsa Fairy
56. Imogen the Ice Dance Fairy

The Sporty Fairies
57. Helena the Horseriding Fairy
58. Francesca the Football Fairy
59. Zoe the Skating Fairy
60. Naomi the Netball Fairy
61. Samantha the Swimming Fairy
62. Alice the Tennis Fairy
63. Gemma the Gymnastics Fairy

The Music Fairies
64. Poppy the Piano Fairy
65. Ellie the Guitar Fairy
66. Fiona the Flute Fairy
67. Danni the Drum Fairy
68. Maya the Harp Fairy
69. Victoria the Violin Fairy
70. Sadie the Saxophone Fairy

The Magical Animal Fairies
71. Ashley the Dragon Fairy ☐
72. Lara the Black Cat Fairy ☐
73. Erin the Firebird Fairy ☐
74. Rihanna the Seahorse Fairy ☐
75. Sophia the Snow Swan Fairy ☐
76. Leona the Unicorn Fairy ☐
77. Caitlin the Ice Bear Fairy ☐

The Green Fairies
78. Nicole the Beach Fairy ☐
79. Isabella the Air Fairy ☐
80. Edie the Garden Fairy ☐
81. Coral the Reef Fairy ☐
82. Lily the Rainforest Fairy ☐
83. Carrie the Snow Cap Fairy ☐
84. Milly the River Fairy ☐

The Ocean Fairies
85. Ally the Dolphin Fairy ☐
86. Amelie the Seal Fairy ☐
87. Pia the Penguin Fairy ☐
88. Tess the Sea Turtle Fairy ☐
89. Stephanie the Starfish Fairy ☐
90. Whitney the Whale Fairy ☐
91. Courtney the Clownfish Fairy ☐

The Twilight Fairies
92. Ava the Sunset Fairy ☐
93. Lexi the Firefly Fairy ☐
94. Zara the Starlight Fairy ☐
95. Morgan the Midnight Fairy ☐
96. Yasmin the Night Owl Fairy ☐
97. Maisie the Moonbeam Fairy ☐
98. Sabrina the Sweet Dreams Fairy ☐

The Showtime Fairies
99. Madison the Magic Show Fairy ☐
100. Leah the Theatre Fairy ☐
101. Alesha the Acrobat Fairy ☐
102. Darcey the Dance Diva Fairy ☐
103. Taylor the Talent Show Fairy ☐
104. Amelia the Singing Fairy ☐
105. Isla the Ice Star Fairy ☐

The Princess Fairies
106. Honor the Happy Days Fairy ☐
107. Demi the Dressing-Up Fairy ☐
108. Anya the Cuddly Creatures Fairy ☐
109. Elisa the Adventure Fairy ☐
110. Lizzie the Sweet Treats Fairy ☐
111. Maddie the Playtime Fairy ☐
112. Eva the Enchanted Ball Fairy ☐

The Pop Star Fairies
113. Jessie the Lyrics Fairy ☐
114. Adele the Singing Coach Fairy ☐
115. Vanessa the Dance Steps Fairy ☐
116. Miley the Stylist Fairy ☐
117. Frankie the Make-Up Fairy ☐
118. Rochelle the Star Spotter Fairy ☐
119. Una the Concert Fairy ☐

The Fashion Fairies
120. Miranda the Beauty Fairy ☐
121. Claudia the Accessories Fairy ☐
122. Tyra the Dress Designer Fairy ☐
123. Alexa the Fashion Reporter Fairy ☐
124. Matilda the Hair Stylist Fairy ☐
125. Brooke the Photographer Fairy ☐
126. Lola the Fashion Fairy ☐

The Sweet Fairies
127. Lottie the Lollipop Fairy ☐
128. Esme the Ice Cream Fairy ☐
129. Coco the Cupcake Fairy ☐
130. Clara the Chocolate Fairy ☐
131. Madeleine the Cookie Fairy ☐
132. Layla the Candyfloss Fairy ☐
133. Nina the Birthday Cake Fairy ☐

The Baby Animal Rescue Fairies
134. Mae the Panda Fairy ☐
135. Kitty the Tiger Fairy ☐
136. Mara the Meerkat Fairy ☐
137. Savannah the Zebra Fairy ☐
138. Kimberley the Koala Fairy ☐
139. Rosie the Honey Bear Fairy ☐
140. Anna the Arctic Fox Fairy ☐

The Magical Crafts Fairies
141. Kayla the Pottery Fairy ☐
142. Annabelle the Drawing Fairy ☐
143. Zadie the Sewing Fairy ☐
144. Josie the Jewellery-Making Fairy ☐
145. Violet the Painting Fairy ☐
146. Libby the Story-Writing Fairy ☐
147. Roxie the Baking Fairy ☐

There's a book of fairy fun for everyone!

www.rainbowmagicbooks.co.uk

Lila & Myla the Twins Fairies

Meet Lila and Myla the Twins Fairies!
Can the fairies stop Jack Frost before he uses
their magic to create his very own twin?

www.rainbowmagicbooks.co.uk